# South East Adventures

### Edited By Machaela Gavaghan

First published in Great Britain in 2018 by:

 Young**Writers**

Young Writers
Remus House
Coltsfoot Drive
Peterborough
PE2 9BF
Telephone: 01733 890066
Website: www.youngwriters.co.uk

# Welcome!

Young Writers was created in 1991 with the express purpose of promoting and encouraging creative writing. Each competition we create is tailored to the relevant age group, hopefully giving each child the inspiration and incentive to create their own piece of work, whether it's a poem or a short story. We truly believe that seeing their stories in print gives pupils a sense of achievement and pride in their work and themselves.

We created *Storyland* for Key Stage 1 pupils to engage them in storytelling, giving them a choice of exciting story maps around which to base their stories. The images give them a framework for their story, allowing them to let their ideas grow and encouraging the use of descriptive language. Through this we hope that the love of literacy will flourish in this next generation of young writers.

Within these pages you will find stories about mermaids and pirates, heroes and villains, ghosts and genies. The children could also choose to write a story without the use of a story map, so there's no limit to the scope of imagination within this collection. Each story showcases the creativity of these budding new writers as they learn the first skills of writing, and we hope you are as entertained by them as we are.

*Jenni Harrison*
Editorial Manager

# Imagine...

We created four unique lands for *Storyland*. Children were shown posters to help inspire them, before using a story map and their imagination to write their own tale. The story maps are on the following pages...

# SCREAMSVILLE

# Contents

## Wendell Park Primary School, London

| | |
|---|---|
| Theo Augustas Compper (7) | 65 |
| Jack Charman Hopkins (7) | 66 |
| Lila Cate Price (7) | 68 |
| Hosna Moradi (7) | 70 |
| Sophia Tuzani (6) | 72 |
| Hana Ikeda-MacDermott (7) | 73 |
| Ishaaq Lakhdari (7) | 74 |
| Yusra Tahir (7) | 75 |
| Riley Philbert (6) | 76 |
| Benjamin Hook | 77 |
| Charlotte Wolsey (7) | 78 |
| Hiyabel Tekle (7) | 79 |
| Noemie Iva Chamoiseau (7) | 80 |
| Albert Clarke (6) | 81 |
| Hannah Mondala (6) | 82 |
| Phoebe Faith Morrow-Okitkpi (7) | 83 |
| Rayan Mohamad (7) | 84 |
| Ben Wood (6) | 85 |
| Kyla Davis (7) | 86 |
| Jayden-Jacq Garry (6) | 87 |

## Yeading Infant & Nursery School, Hayes

| | |
|---|---|
| Arham B Nomani (6) | 88 |
| Sruthiga Sivakantharuban (6) | 90 |
| Yuvika Thapa (6) | 92 |
| Manreet Kaur (7) | 94 |
| Dima Al-Shammari (6) | 95 |
| Girish Ganger (6) | 96 |
| Gurnoor Kaur (6) | 97 |
| Fateh Singh Hansra (6) | 98 |
| Asmitha Vasavan (6) | 99 |
| Armaan Singh Bagri (6) | 100 |
| Aaliyah N Balogun (7) | 101 |
| Ayshnavi Vinojan (6) | 102 |
| Hibaq Ali (7) | 103 |
| Piranuyan Ketheeswaran (6) | 104 |
| Naveen Sasikaran (7) | 105 |
| Maheen Saeed (5) | 106 |
| Gunwant Kaur Sandhu (6) | 107 |
| Eshanya Kaur Khaneja (7) | 108 |

| | |
|---|---|
| Tahmeed Ahmed (7) | 109 |
| Akash Suresh (7) | 110 |
| Roopkamal Kaur (7) | 111 |
| Simrat Sandhar (7) | 112 |
| Rosan Sureshkumar (7) | 113 |
| Khalid Yusuf Mursal (6) | 114 |
| Varun Sriyen Loganayayam (6) | 115 |
| Parampreet Singh Gill (7) | 116 |
| Hafsah Khalid (7) | 117 |
| Adam Di Pietra (6) | 118 |
| Kavish Mohanachselvan (6) | 119 |
| Avaneesh Punniyaseelan (6) | 120 |
| Mubak Omar (6) | 121 |
| Talha Kashif (7) | 122 |
| Mnsy Shafiq (5) | 123 |
| Manraj Singh (7) | 124 |
| Ayan Ranjit (7) | 125 |
| Anastazja Stanisz (6) | 126 |
| Akshera Thurairajah (5) | 127 |
| Samuel Adebambo Balogunezzedine (6) | 128 |
| Wajih Khan (6) | 129 |
| Daniyal Ali Rana (7) | 130 |
| Desmond Akanmu (7) | 131 |
| Moulid Abdi Osman (7) | 132 |

# The Stories

# The Superheroes Save The Day!

Once, there lived three superheroes. The biggest one was shaped like a butterfly and her name was Ice. The middle one was like a worm and his name was Flash. The third one was called Geko. On the moon lived the evil mastermind. His name was Brain Sorcerer. His plan was to rule the world and control everyone's minds! But Brain could be stopped by the superheroes and he would be gone forever.

One dark, windy evening when Geko was sleeping, Brain caught her and took her to the secret lair! After he caught Geko, Brain put her into a glass bottle and took her powers.

When it was done, the glass started to fill with purple water. Suddenly, Geko looked left and right. There she saw her friends, Flash and Ice. Flash used his speed, broke the glass and saved Geko. After that, Flash, Geko and Ice pushed the evil Brain into the bottle so he could never get out. Finally, Candy Land was safe again!

## Autumn Alana Grace Greenaway (7)

Chesterfield Primary School, Enfield

# The Incredible Superheroes!

Long ago in a land far, far away, lived two superheroes. One was called Butterfly Girl. She was the tallest and could make butterflies attack bad guys. The other one was called Yellow Wi-Fi. Her power was to make Wi-Fi balls and throw them at the villains. If you didn't know, Wi-Fi balls zap mean creatures.

In a galaxy not far away, the evil mastermind Crang was secretly planning to rule the world, including Candy Land, the land of candy and superheroes.

One stormy night, Butterfly Girl was strolling along the path when she saw something silver shining and hovering about in the sky. As she was trying to spread her wings, they got stuck! Crang lowered down a little bit and grabbed her by the hair and flew off with her. The next thing she knew, she found herself in a see-through jar.

A moment later, Crang decided to take her powers by placing his tentacles on her head. The next minute, the jar started to fill up with pink, purple and golden lava. Butterfly Girl was petrified! The colourful lava was halfway. Butterfly Girl thought she was going to die! Just then, she heard zaps and glanced and scanned the room.

It was her best friend, Yellow Wi-Fi! She shot her Wi-Fi balls at Crang and then she immediately freed Butterfly Girl. She was safe at last! But, it wasn't quite the end, Butterfly Girl grabbed Crang and Yellow Wi-Fi shot more balls at him. Butterfly Girl swooped to the jar and pushed him in!

## Sofia Emily Lillieth Semper (7)
Chesterfield Primary School, Enfield

# Katelin's Heroes' Hideout Story

Firstly, this story is about some heroes that travel around the universe and amazing world, fighting villains and saving the world. But everybody wonders how they always win! People discovered they team up and that's how they always win. Of course, by being a team.

Soon, the cruel, disgusting, mean alien planned to rule the world, even though he knew the superheroes were going to stop him, but he had a plan. Since they worked together, the evil alien decided to split them up. Then, the superheroes heard that the alien wanted to rule the world. They were very cross but they didn't know his plan. The foolish, evil alien saw only one superhero and quickly just grabbed her. He flew away, only splitting up one superhero.

After that, he kept her in a dangerous, sharp, glass cage. She was extremely bored, sleep and angry. Before long, the superheroes were captured. The alien made her talk but she wouldn't tell him anything. She thought about it and she thought about her team. They were more than a team, they were friends, they were family. Her friends came to rescue her, they got out as quick as a flash!

Finally, they left, they came back and put the alien where they'd found their teammate!

## Katelin Dias (7)

Highbury Quadrant Primary School, London

# Rae-Marie's Enchanted Island Story

Once upon a time far, far away, there was a beautiful princess called Isabel. It was her birthday, she was going to be thirteen. What she really wanted for her birthday was a unicorn so she asked her mum if she could have a unicorn.

The next day, she woke up and got dressed and went downstairs to eat her breakfast. Then, a van came with a very huge parcel for pretty Isabel. When she opened it, she couldn't believe her eyes. It was her pink and white unicorn!

After that, Isabel, her mum, dad, brother and her baby sister started to get the party ready. For the food, they had delicious sandwiches, yummy pizza, fantastic home-made pineapple jelly and a fantastic chocolate cake.

Soon, all her princess and prince friends were there. They each had a present and a card for her. When they came into the castle, they couldn't believe their eyes! They'd never seen a castle this beautiful. They shouted, "We love it!" Isabel was about to say a speech but then a monster came to destroy the party because he was trying to have a nap so he needed some peace.

Finally, the brave, intelligent knight came and scared the monster away. Isabel and her friends and family lived happily ever after.

## Rae-Marie Lewis-Charles (7)

Highbury Quadrant Primary School, London

# Yasmine's Screamsville Story

Firstly, there was a boy called Christopher and it was his first time trick or treating and he had the most sweets. He said to his lovely, caring mum, "I want to go trick or treating every day!"

Secondly, he went to school. Of course, he went trick or treating and when he went to people's houses, they looked strange so he said to the stranger, "I told myself I should go trick or treating." Christopher went to the next house but nothing was strange, they just gave him candy and then turned into a ghost! Christopher dropped the sweet, delicious candy. Suddenly, there appeared Bloody Mary, then the zombies and Christopher ran home. Even Christopher's parents turned into ghosts and zombies, it was awful and horrible! Christopher had found a book full of magic spells. He tried to reverse the spell and turn all the things back to normal.

Finally, they had a disco for reversing the spell and helping other people and doing the chores. Christopher learnt his lesson - not to go trick or treating when it's not Halloween.

## Yasmine Mouzaoui (7)
Highbury Quadrant Primary School, London

# The Screaming

There once was a small, tiny boy called Bobby.
Bobby thought he was super-duper brave.
However, he was not! He once went into a haunted
house and got frightened.

Firstly, he took a couple of steps and heard an
*oooh* noise so he got even more scared. Secondly,
he found a locked door, Bobby was also very
curious so he knocked on the door and the door
opened. Inside, he saw creepy zombies, mummies
with huge shadows and annoying vampires! As
soon as his brain started working again, he ran
and ran but the annoying, dumb and ugly
monsters wanted to eat him.

After running and running, he realised that he was
faster than all of them. Suddenly, out of nowhere,
the king zombie rose up from the ground. He was
huge, green, damp and could run quickly. Bobby
was as fast as a shiny race car so he got ahead of
the king zombie.

Finally, he got to his home sweet home, but he had
no sweets. But it didn't matter because his mum
had a secret stash so they all had a party!

## Faheem Mohmad (6)
Highbury Quadrant Primary School, London

# Blue Lagoon

Once upon a time, there lived an adventurous, young mermaid called Beautiful Mermaid. She had a sparkly tail that could light up in the dark and she was eight years old.

Before that, the anxious mermaid played with her amazing, lovely friends and she swam as fast as the waves so she could give delicious food to the colourful fish and the other interesting mermaids.

After, a white, smooth, fantastic mermaid saw a kind boy drowning. Mermaid said, "Oh no!" So the shy mermaid put him on the clean, shiny boat and he came to life.

The boy said, "Thank you!" The amazing mermaid made him a tiny, splendid bed with a gold crown. He really liked it.

Meanwhile, the excited mermaid and a handsome boy went outside and they swam. Also, they waved at the incredible octopuses, they waved back quickly.

After, the mermaid said, "I am so happy!"

The confident boy said, "My name is Billy."

## Maryam Kalam (7)
Highbury Quadrant Primary School, London

# Olivia's Blue Lagoon Story

Once, there lived a mermaid called Lily. She loved being a mermaid. She enjoyed playing with the dolphins but the sharks were scary, but one shark was nice. They were a bit scared of the shark but they soon became friends.

After, she swam to shore. She saw a huge boat, it had evil pirates on it. Then, the pirates took her! She tried to swim away but she couldn't. She tried and tried but she could not do it! "I am missing my friends so much!" She was so sad for her friends but there was a surfer who saved her from the pirates!

Before half an hour, the surfer came to take her away from the pirates. Suddenly, he jumped onto the boat. He grabbed her and took her into the ocean. They played with each other and she loved it.

Finally, she went home, got some dinner and went to bed.

## Olivia Taylor (7)
Highbury Quadrant Primary School, London

# Sahara's Blue Lagoon Story

On a bright, sunny afternoon, Milly the mermaid was talking to Milan the seahorse about the mermaid kingdom and all the cool stuff she'd found underwater. She dreamt of being a human and walking on dry land.

So one day, Milly made a deal with a squid called Pirate Pete. He said he would make her human in exchange for her voice. He secretly lied. Milly said, "Okay!"

"Climb on board!" Pete said. He got her to sign a contract. "Haha! It's a trick! You're coming with me."

"Wait, what?"

A handsome surfer was surfing and he saw Milly, then he decided to save her. He climbed onto the ship and pushed the pirate off!

Finally, they swam to shore and Milly thanked the surfer for saving her.

## Sahara Kalu (7)

Highbury Quadrant Primary School, London

# Aoki-Lee's Screamsville Story

Once upon a time, there lived a sweet little boy named Alex. He was picking out a costume for Halloween. He wore a vampire costume.

Next, Alex went trick or treating on the street and saw a creepy house. It was scary and dark but he seemed to like it so he went in it. Then, there was a zombie behind him but Alex didn't know so he kept on walking into the house. He said, "What is this house?" After that, there were no treats outside the door so Alex went in it. "Come out whoever you are!" Soon, he saw all the monsters but he was happy because they were nice and Alex even became a vampire!

Finally, they had a party on Saturday and they were friends forever, but Alex never went home!

## Aoki-Lee Appiah (6)
Highbury Quadrant Primary School, London

# Jalil's Heroes' Hideout

Firstly, a hero came! Next, there were four more supersonic heroes with two jetpack lasers. Then, all the jetpack lasers needed new lasers. After, they needed to be put down for a hundred hours. Meanwhile, a troll came and the troll made the superhero transform with a magic wand. They needed to fight the ugly troll! The grumpy troll grabbed the good-looking girl, then the girl got taken away for good. Then, the troll came back. After that, the girl got tied up in a tight, not nice rope. The heroes came to rescue the lovely, nice, cute girl. The girl was rescued by the lovely superheroes! The heroes got the ugly troll and then they hid it and had a nice day!

## Jalil Gordon (7)
Highbury Quadrant Primary School, London

# Gabriella's Screamsville Story

Once upon a time, there was a banned town called Screamsville. It had Bloody Mary, Baby Blue and Candy Man. Everyone who used to live there had memories of almost getting hurt. Now, vampires live in Screamsville. They own the place! I know this myself because I still live here in Screamsville, as well as my best friend Sahara. Anyways, I'm here to tell you kid, teen or adult, look around this horrid town of screams and tricks. Firstly, in the unkind town of Screamsville, there's a portal to escape. Next, you can turn evil to trick Bloody Mary.

Finally, do you know the town has eyes? Wherever you go, the eyes can guide you. Screamsville is in England.

## Gabriella Marques (7)

Highbury Quadrant Primary School, London

# Yasir's Heroes' Hideout Story

There were two random superheroes that saved the day from baddies. Fifty-six bad people were taking people's money. The bad people mind-controlled the city and also the superheroes. But then, the superheroes kicked open the door very hard and then it opened.

After a while, they stopped fighting because they wanted to go home. The superheroes went to sleep.

After a while, they heard bad guys attacking the world but they got lasers to help them and they had their friends with them. They used their lasers to fight the bad guys and then came a strong superhero and he went home when he'd finished fighting the bad people. Then he ate some spaghetti.

## Yasir Salam (7)

Highbury Quadrant Primary School, London

# Zombie Failure Attack Let-Down

Once upon a time, there were zombies that once ran out of food. How they survived nobody knows but it is said that they shared some brains and blood and travelled back to HQPS - Highbury Quadrant Primary School. Then they came back to get more blood and brains from somewhere but someone had a plan. It was Malacky the Wise. His plan was to set a zombie trap. It was then that a zombie stepped in it and got caught. Then, they could ask it some questions about its plan so they could stop it.

After, they put these traps around the school. That stopped the zombies from coming and stealing people's brains and blood. "Please don't return now!"

## Dylan Pelter Gilbody (7)

Highbury Quadrant Primary School, London

# Angus' Screamsville Story

Once upon a time, there were some ordinary kids that lived in a cement and brick house. They went on a walk on a cold, dark night but just then, a mysterious portal appeared and they got into the strange object and found themselves on a strange land. The land was full of ghosts and skeletons and extraterrestrials. Then, they got caught by a skeleton! They got their knives and chopped him up, then they found 2,000 skeletons surrounding them! They had swords, bows and arrows. Finally, they defeated them and the normal kids picked up all the pointy weapons and went home.

## Angus Milne (7)
Highbury Quadrant Primary School, London

# The Dog's Big Bone

Once upon a time, there lived a thoughtful, nice dog called Amber and she liked bones.

One day, she went on a walk. Soon after, while she was walking on the bumpy road, she spotted another dog with a big bone.

Eventually, she pounced on the dog because she really, really wanted it.

Soon after, she was walking away with a huge bone in her mouth! It was as huge as a boulder! Meanwhile, her master, Miss Bobbleboots, was really worried because she couldn't find her dog! Finally, Amber came back with the big bone and Miss Bobbleboots was shocked.

## Aimee Shah (7)
Highbury Quadrant Primary School, London

# Mermaid Lost In The Sea

First, there was a beautiful, good-looking mermaid in the sea. She was just sunbathing, enjoying her day.

One day, a ship came with an octopus pirate. It was very twitchy and a little bit ugly but the boat was cute. The pirate wasn't nice. He was a kidnapper and he kidnapped the mermaid and put her in the dungeon!

After a few hours, a little boy came surfing and saw the poor mermaid crying on the ship. He saved the sad mermaid. He had a crown and put it on her head, then that was the end of the pirate. They married each other and lived happily ever after.

**Tamar Niamh Watson (7)**
Highbury Quadrant Primary School, London

# Yasir's Heroes' Hideout Story

Once upon a time, there were some crazy superheroes and some bad villains. They were going to take over the world so the heroes needed to help. "We need a plan."
"Like what?"
"To save the world so there won't be any villains!" One of them went.
"Wait!" said the others but she went.
"Come on!"
When they went... *bam!* "He is the enemy!" She was being controlled by his brain. His main power didn't work. She came out, she looked amazing. She put the enemy inside!

## Yasir Uddin (6)
Highbury Quadrant Primary School, London

# The Old Turtle And His Friends

Once, there was an enormous turtle who lived in a house hidden under rocks in the reef with all the scary stuff. However, he had a few friends. I can tell you, they were all like him. They always swam around like tiny, stupid babies. They always got lost, then they just found their way home to one of their houses.

After, they went around celebrating because they'd found their way back home. They celebrated all day and night too, enjoying the spectacular harbours.

Finally, as you know, friendships are never broken.

## Alex Byrne (7)

Highbury Quadrant Primary School, London

# They Found A Lamp

There was a girl and her name was Jasmine. There was a boy called Lord.

One day, they found a magic lamp. They thought it was a king but the girl said, "Look, it is a kind lamp!" Then they just rubbed the lamp and out came... "What? A genie! What shall we do?" They rubbed it until the lamp went back to normal. The genie went back into the lamp. Well, they saved the door! They broke the lamp.

## Aybuke Nar Yildiz (7)

Highbury Quadrant Primary School, London

# Yasmin's Enchanted Island Story

One starry night, there was a lot of stars in the sky. On this beautiful night, along came two children, a little girl named Britney and a boy named David. They both loved to fight. They even went to karate classes and they loved it there.

All of a sudden on this beautiful night, Britney and David stumbled upon a lamp, they both looked at each other wondering if the lamp was real or fake. They both said, "I think it is real." Britney and David couldn't believe their eyes! So they both decided to rub the lamp. In a hurry out of nowhere, a genie came out of the lamp and decided to create his own world, he decided to take down the magical castle. While he was doing that, he smelt delicious smoke above him.

David said to Britney, "We must stop him and put him back into the lamp."

The genie heard them both so he decided to have a war with Britney and David. Britney and David won the war and defeated the extreme, terrible genie.

David and Britney lived happily ever after but before they did all of that, they put the genie back into the lamp and buried him so no one could find him.

## Yasmin Rachid Saidi (7)

Honilands Primary School, Enfield

# Cinar's Storyland Adventure

Once upon a time on an enchanted island, there lived a king and queen.

One day, an evil monster stole the king's crown, then threw the crown into the sea. He was laughing!

The next morning, the king woke up. He put his clothes on but he saw the crown had gone. He was so mad! The knight came to the king's room and couldn't find the crown. The knight thought the king wasn't the real king, then the knight said, "Put your hands up!"

The king said, "No, I am the real king."

"No, you are the fake king! You are going to prison," said the knight.

"No, I am not going to prison," said the king. The knight called 999, then the police officer came.

At night-time, the knight put some cameras in the king's bedroom. When the monster came back to steal his stuff, the knight saw who had stolen the crown so he called 999 again. The knight said, "I need the ring back, please."

## Cinar Karamugara (7)
Honilands Primary School, Enfield

# Kwadwo's Storyland Adventure

One night, a boy called Joe was daydreaming when a teleporter came into his face. The teleporter said, "You will be sent to an enchanted island." Immediately, he got teleported to the enchanted island and he woke up. It seemed weird. Out of nowhere, a fire soldier came into Joe's face.

The fire soldier said, "Want to use my transforming vehicle? It shoots out missiles and if we want to rule the world, we can destroy that castle where the king and queen live." So they went in the jet and they both destroyed the king and queen's castle. All of a sudden, the king and queen's crown had disappeared. They were really angry because their castle was destroyed.

In a hurry, the fire soldier, Joe, said, "What shall we do?" *Let's build them a new everything.* And they did.

## Kwadwo Owusu-Ansah (7)
Honilands Primary School, Enfield

# Kennedy's Enchanted Island Story

Once upon a time, there lived Elsa and Kristoff, heroes of the enchanted island. They were going on a quest to find a genie to grant them arrows. The horse was galloping and Elsa was walking until they found something. They stumbled across a golden lamp. They dug it up, then they did something they shouldn't have done - they rubbed the lamp! Out of nowhere, a genie popped up out of the lamp. "What is this creature?" It stamped through the forest, to the castle but it fell in the gigantic castle! It screamed loud. He'd never fallen in a castle before. He wanted to destroy it for himself. Elsa and Kristoff heard the crash and rushed to the castle. Immediately, they began battling the genie. Elsa and Kristoff won, then buried him so no one would ever find him again.

**Kennedy Maslen-Street (6)**
Honilands Primary School, Enfield

# Ayesha's Enchanted Island Story

Once upon a time on an enchanted island, there were two brave knights called Mary, who was the best at using the bow and arrow, and Peter, who was a courageous knight.

One early morning, Mary and Peter travelled on a journey into the shimmering, emerald forest. Immediately, they discovered a mysterious lamp. They rubbed the lamp vigorously. They asked, "Where did this come from?" The genie came out of a delicious puff. In a hurry, he escaped and started to create a mess. He got his axe and started to crash down the castle. They rushed and had a battle. Mary used her bow and arrow and Peter used his sword to defeat the genie. They caught the genie and put him in his lamp and buried him in the mud so that he couldn't ever come out of his lamp.

## Ayesha Abdifatah Ahmed (7)
Honilands Primary School, Enfield

# Eric's Enchanted Island Story

One starry night, Amy, the best bow and arrow shooter, and Alex, the best, bravest knight, were going through an enormous forest after they'd seen each other and teamed up to find a lamp so they could be rich. Amy and Alex tripped over a gold, beaming lamp buried in the wet, musky mud. In a hurry, Alex and Amy rubbed the lamp at the same time. There came a giant genie! Immediately, Alex and Amy asked, "What are you?" Then he got mad and destroyed the castle by getting an axe. All of a sudden they shouted, "You're a beast!" At the beginning, they believed that they couldn't fight it. Amy tried to fight it with a bow and arrow whilst Alex created a magic sword.

They finally defeated the genie. After, they had a celebration!

## Eric Botezatu (7)

Honilands Primary School, Enfield

# Joyce's Enchanted Island Story

Once upon a time on an enchanted island, there was a boy and a girl called Zania and Ben. They worked together as a team. To get ready, they trained.

One splendid day when they were walking through the emerald forest, they spotted something beaming on the ground. It was a magical lamp! They asked, "What is this lamp?" Immediately, they wanted to see what was inside. They rubbed the lamp immediately and in a delicious, creative puff of smoke, a genie escaped out of the lamp. In a hurry, the genie ran to the castle and destroyed the fabulous castle! Zania and Ben had a battle with the genie and Zania caught him. He disappeared back into the lamp. Now they had found out how rude he was, they buried the genie deep down in the mud forever!

## Joyce Massamba-Mianda (7)
Honilands Primary School, Enfield

# Melanie's Storyland Adventure

One day, there was a beautiful rainbow princess. She was on an island, then a scary dragon came and took the princess to a volcano. In a hurry, she used her power, then the dragon fell into the volcano and it erupted. The dragon flew onto the trampoline next to the volcano. The dragon turned rainbow, then the dragon pounced up and down, then he saw a sparkly, green dinosaur cake and a white, butterfly princess cake. They ate the cakes and the trophy went to the princess and she got a medal. She put it in her bedroom. She brought her princess friends and they were doing an acrobat show. People came to see the show, then they had a party and danced and had food and drinks.

**Melanie Cabral Tavares (6)**
Honilands Primary School, Enfield

# Sameera's Storyland Adventure

Once upon a time, there was a brave princess called Macy. She lived in a beautiful palace on an enchanted island.

One day when Macy was in the city, a big, angry dragon grabbed her and took the princess to his ugly tower.

When Macy was in the tall tower, she was trying to break out of the huge chains so she used her bow and arrow, then climbed down the dusty tower quickly. The amazed princess had a party. They had fun and she liked playing with her four friends, Stacey, Amy, Lilah and Sky.

When it was Wednesday, she went to bow and arrow class and stayed there for six hours.

Finally, she watched some television at the palace.

## Sameera Inioluwa Oyedokun (6)

Honilands Primary School, Enfield

# Deszon's Heroes' Hideout Story

Once upon a time, there were five superheroes. They had magic powers and they were brave and strong.

One day, there was an evil villain. His name was Claw. He wanted to take over the world! He was mean and scary, everyone was scared of him. The superheroes chased the bad villain when he took a superhero with his big, black claw! He whizzed through the sky. The evil villain put the hero in a hard cage and she was trapped forever! What would she do? Suddenly, her superhero friends appeared. *Zap! Crash! Bang!* They broke the glass case, it smashed.

Finally, he got trapped in the cage forever and ever! Everyone was safe.

## Deszon Chijanma (6)

Honilands Primary School, Enfield

# Alexia's Storyland Adventure

Once upon a time lived a king and a princess. When the king woke up, he was shocked because his crown was gone. The night before, a messy, tall troll quietly jumped through the window and stole the crown from a blue, magical chest.

The king went on a hunt to find the troll. He found him in a cave but it was blocked up with a big rock so nobody could get in. All of a sudden, the rock moved and the troll came out. Sneakily, the king crept into the troll's cave because he wanted his crown back. The king found his crown under the troll's smelly bed. Carefully, the king took the crown and ran away, back to his castle.

## Alexia Hajinicolaou (6)
Honilands Primary School, Enfield

# Selin's Heroes' Hideout Story

Once upon a time, there were five brave and strong superheroes. They whizzed around the busy city to see if there were bad villains.

One day, the spider claw planned to take over the world. He was evil and unkind to people. Oh no, the spider claw took Supergirl to his secret hideout. He whizzed in the dark sky, holding her tightly. The spider claw locked her in a glass cage and kept her forever and ever! Suddenly, her friends appeared. They bashed and banged the glass cage. They saved her from the evil villain! Finally, they caught the spider claw and locked him away. Everyone was safe!

## Selin Kole Patel (6)

Honilands Primary School, Enfield

# Reece's Heroes' Hideout Story

Once, in a city called The Valley, there were five superheroes called Jake, Katey, Max, Maxy and Jacky.

Once in space, there was an alien called Mr Bad Pants and he lived on a planet called The Wheel. Then, he decided he was going to Earth. He zoomed to Earth and he grabbed Maxy, he flew back home.

When he got home, he tied Maxy up and put Maxy in an ice-cold glass cage. "Oh no! What am I going to do?" Then, her superhero friends came to save her, she said, "Yay!" Then, they put Mr Bad Pants in the ice-cold glass cage. The superheroes saved the day!

## Reece Wright (6)
Honilands Primary School, Enfield

# Kelsey's Heroes' Hideout Story

Once upon a time, there were five superheroes who whizzed around the sky saving the world. They were brave and strong.

One day, the spider claw tried to take over the world. He was evil and not nice to anyone.

One day, the spider claw took the superhero! Oh no, what would they do? The spider claw locked her in a smooth glass cage where she couldn't use her powers. Suddenly, her superhero friends appeared and *zap!* The glass smashed into pieces. *Boom!*

Finally, they had got the spider claw where he could stay forever! The world was safe.

## Kelsey Tadgell (6)
Honilands Primary School, Enfield

# Jeyda's Heroes' Hideout Story

Once upon a time, there were five superheroes. They helped people that were in trouble. They were brave and kind. The evil villain called Brainiac wanted to take over the world. Brainiac was powerful and crazy. Brainiac took a princess to his evil lab. He trapped her in a cage. Brainiac felt happy because his plan was working very well. The princess felt sad. *Bam! Crash! Boom!* Suddenly, the five superheroes came to Brainiac's lab. They saved the princess! The superheroes trapped Brainiac. He felt sad and the superheroes lived happily ever after.

## Jeyda Hassan (6)
Honilands Primary School, Enfield

# Cecilia's Heroes' Hideout Story

One day in the city, there were four superheroes and their names were Flash, Owlet, Geko and Nilen and they saved the world. The slimy alien was making a plan to destroy the world. Owlet was using her powers but the slimy alien was too fast. Owlet was stuck in a case and she was sad because she thought she would be stuck there forever. Owlet was happy now because her superhero friends saved her. *Crash! Boom! Zap! Wham!* Nilen and Flash put the slimy alien in the case. The villain used her laser eyes so that she could see people.

## Cecilia Nimbo (6)
Honilands Primary School, Enfield

# Ela's Storyland Adventure

One day, there was a princess. The princess needed help. Her sister was lost! She told the king, the king said to come there. The lost princess had a pink dress. The knight came and found her, she was in the forest. Her sister was crying because she was not well. They called for a car to go to the castle.

When they came to the princess, she was shocked. The princess hugged her sister.

Soon, the sick princess died. The big sister had a wedding and a baby girl and her mum came to the hospital with her sister!

## Ela Kubat (6)

Honilands Primary School, Enfield

# Abdikaliq's Heroes' Hideout Story

Once upon a time, there were five superheroes. One was called Vioeer. Vioeer was the leader. The evil villain was on a building, he wanted to rule the world. The evil villain took one of them. She cried, "Help!" No one answered. He took her away to his cave. The evil villain trapped her in an electric cage. What could she do? Suddenly, her friends teleported with a *pow!* They smashed the glass. Finally, they trapped the villain with their superpowers.

## Abdikaliq B (5)

Honilands Primary School, Enfield

# Nathan's Heroes' Hideout Story

In the deep city, there were five heroes called Cara, Meo, Avogo, Sama and Rumbo. There was an alien called Shadow Man. He lived on Planet of Nails because his bed was made of nails. "Oh no! Sama has been taken by Shadow Man!" He swooped and he had laser eyes. Shadow Man had gone crazy. He put her in a glass cage and made her a villain. Soon, her friends came to rescue her from Shadow Man. They put Shadow Man in there so they could turn him into a good guy.

## Nathan Newman (6)
Honilands Primary School, Enfield

# Adele's Heroes' Hideout Story

One night, there were five superheroes and they saved the day and they had superpowers. They heard something from the sky and it was a villain. It took one superhero! The villain grabbed her and she said, "Help!" No one heard her, she was sad. The villain got his revenge. He put her in a glass case and he took her powers. Suddenly, her friends came and got her superpowers and they saved the world. The villain was sad and they put him in the glass case.

## Adele Danso (6)
Honilands Primary School, Enfield

# Kayne's Heroes' Hideout Story

Once upon a time, there were five superheroes. They were brave and strong and they were saving the world.

One sunny day, a monster wanted to get a superhero to get all the powers so he could rule the world! The monster got a superhero and got her in his cave. She tried to get out but she couldn't, she was sad. Supergirl couldn't use her powers! The superheroes came. *Zap!* The cage opened and she was saved. Everyone was safe and sound.

## Kayne Nathan Dorsamy Payen (5)
Honilands Primary School, Enfield

# Fatima's Heroes' Hideout Story

Once upon a time, there were five superheroes. They were all brave and strong. They had superpowers.

One day, the claw wanted to take over the world. He was unkind and mean.

One day, he took Supergirl with his brown claw. Oh no, he put her in a glass cage! He kept her there and took her powers. *Bang! Zoom! Crash!*

Suddenly, her friends came and they saved her! Then he was stuck in the glass cage forever.

## Fatima Zahra (6)

Honilands Primary School, Enfield

# The Bay Of The Bird

In a land far away, there was a house. In that house, there was a child. The child went on a boat to The Bay of the Bird, the mysterious place that no one had ever been to.

When she got there, a magic door appeared. She opened it and a phoenix swooped out and said, "Welcome to The Bay of the Bird."

"Wow!" shouted the girl.

Inside The Bay of the Bird, there was a palace. That was the phoenix's palace. All the birds of the bay loved her, but the phoenix needed help. The bird catcher was hunting them so the girl went off to find him. She went off determinedly because the bird catcher was her evil uncle, Raynor.

When she found him, she found birdcages everywhere. "Give me back my beautiful birds!" she shouted.

"Never!" he shouted so she called the phoenix and they distracted him while the others helped the birds out of their cages and locked him in!

"See how he likes it!" the girl laughed.

## Alyanna Cadby (7)
St Dominic's RC Primary School, London

# The Myths Of The Enchanted Knights And Archery Girl

One magical morning, there was a girl who loved archery. She was known as Archery Princess. She loved archery in her life more than anything else. One fascinating morning, she met a brave and courageous knight. He was called Shining Armour the Brave.

One day, they went to a beautiful place but suddenly, they saw something glowing gold. It was a mystical lamp. They were amazed at what they saw but they didn't know what to do with it. Archery Princess and Shining Armour the Brave were scared.

After five minutes, eventually, in a puff of smoke, a genie appeared but Archery Princess and Shining Armour the Brave didn't know what it was. They followed it to know what it actually was for five days. They bought everything and slept under the stars. Suddenly, he was in Archery Princess' home castle of archery. He was actually trying to use his axe to cut down the castle! Both Archery Princess and Shining Armour the Brave tried to defeat the giant but it was no use, the giant said in an evil voice, "Mwahaha, you will never win!"

But when he turned his back, Archery Princess got the lamp and transported him back.
Finally, they lived a happy life. Archery Princess buried the lamp and lived happily ever after.

## De-Shornae Naveah Ming (7)

St Dominic's RC Primary School, London

# The Pirate Octopus And The Mermaid Princess

Once upon a time, there was a mermaid princess who lived in a beautiful castle at the bottom of the sea.

One day, the mermaid princess came up to the surface to look at her treasure in the cave. The mermaid princess saw a pirate ship coming towards the shore where she was sitting. The mermaid princess looked so afraid of the pirate ship that she wanted to go back into the water. It was Octopus Pirate, he grabbed the mermaid princess and her treasure. The mermaid princess shouted for help. Russean and his turtle friend, Ron, saw the mermaid princess at the bottom of the octopus' pirate ship, looking so unhappy. Russean and Ron went over to help her. Russean and Ron talked to the octopus pirate to let the mermaid princess go. The octopus pirate agreed to let the mermaid princess and her treasure go. The octopus pirate wasn't very happy about his talk with Russean and Ron but the octopus pirate said, "Ah, a pirate always keeps his words." He sailed away.

The mermaid princess, Russean and Ron were best friends forever and happy to play at sea.

## Dylan White-Thompson (5)

St Dominic's RC Primary School, London

# The Enchanted War

One day, there lived a little girl with a bow and arrow that played in the park with a boy with a unicorn. They saw a glowing thing on the ground. They went to pick it up. It was a genie bottle! They rushed it open. All of a sudden, a giant genie jumped up and did a cackle. Heart beating fast he said, "Now I can rule the world and take the humans!" He laughed.

"Oh no humans, I need to go! Let me hide behind the castle. Oh no, I'm too big!"

Unicorn Boy said, "Bow and arrow girl, shoot!"

*Pish! Whoosh!*

"Ouch!" said the girl. Genie pushed himself onto the floor.

"Yes, we defeated him! Now let's hide this thing so no one finds it."

"Okay." Did they really defeat him?

## Chidinma Adindu (6)

St Dominic's RC Primary School, London

# Lucy-May And The Giant

Once upon a time, there was a girl and a boy. The boy was called Joshua and the girl was called Lucy-May. Lucy-May had an arrow and her brother had a beautiful horse.

One day, Lucy-May found a lamp in the sand. They looked at it and they thought it was a genie inside. As they looked inside, the lamp began to glow, then a magical genie came out and wanted to be very, very, very bad and naughty. The genie got angry and tried to chop down a very big, beautiful castle. After, the bad genie tried to get Lucy-May and Joshua. Lucy-May scared the bad genie and Joshua and Lucy-May fought the bad genie. They both defeated the bad genie. The bad genie never returned to the kingdom again and Joshua and Lucy-May never saw a genie again in their lives!

## Annabel Folorunsho (5)

St Dominic's RC Primary School, London

# Javonte's Enchanted Island Story

Two girlfriends, Kat and Jean, were in a large forest. Kat was riding a strong horse and Jean was standing with an arrow in her hand. They both looked over and saw a genie lamp. Jean suggested that they should rub the lamp to see if the genie would come out. A very strong Chinese genie came out of the lamp and they were surprised. Kat wished they had a castle to protect them from the genie called Solomon. They began to battle. Jean shot her bow and arrow at the genie while Kat used her sword and hit away Solomon's axe. They were so happy when the genie fell to the ground and disappeared into the gold lamp...

## Javonte Barrow (5)
St Dominic's RC Primary School, London

# The Knight And The Princess

One day, there was a brave knight who saw a cute princess. Later, they became friends. Suddenly, the cute princess dropped so she cried and the knight was really worried.

After, the cute princess and the brave knight saw a magical, golden, shiny lamp. Magically, the genie fastly came out of the lamp, zooming to the cute princess and the brave knight.

After, the genie turned into a bad genie! The genie was about to smash the palace. The bad genie was about to use a sword and break the princess' leg but then the knight broke the bad genie's leg. Finally, they lived happily ever after.

## Solomon Osei (7)

St Dominic's RC Primary School, London

# Odelia's Enchanted Island Story

Astonishingly, an enchanting princess was playing with her young brother. She had a bow and arrow and her brother had a sword, it was their favourite game. They found a shiny, shimmering lamp, then they rubbed it carefully and made a wish and their wishes came true! Then, a genie appeared from the shimmering, shiny lamp. The genie was very rude. The genie was destroying the castle and the boy and the girl ran out of the castle, the genie was enormous! The unicorn boy defeated the genie with the prince. They were happy and they never made another wish.

## Odelia Oghenemega Udi (7)
St Dominic's RC Primary School, London

# The Little Mermaid

Once, there was a mermaid in the deep ocean. The mermaid was hunting for some shells. She was a teenager. She was scared because a pirate ship sank to the bottom, right in front of her home. There was a mean octopus. Octopus grabbed her hand, the mermaid started to cry. She saw a golden charm and asked, "Where did you get the charm from?"

A surfer saw the mermaid at the bottom and helped her. He had a turtle and rescued her. The octopus was angry and mad. The mermaid took a crown that had crystals and was glowing.

## Nicole Farrugia (7)

St Dominic's RC Primary School, London

# Isaac's Screamsville Story

One day, a boy named Josh was a vampire for Halloween. He went trick or treating. He got lots of sweets, they were yummy. He came to a spooky house. It had bats that were screeching out of the dark shadows. It was weird in the dark night.

Next, he was walking towards the spooky house. Behind him, a monster was following him. Heart beating fast, eyes popping out, out of nowhere, the door opened. He went in and monsters snuck in and popped up. It was scary!

Finally, it was a disco party because there was a disco light!

## Isaac Shitta (7)

St Dominic's RC Primary School, London

# The Gold River

One hot, sunny day, the man was riding on a horse that was riding very slowly and his name was Mike. He was riding to a girl called Ariam. He said about the island and then they went to the island and inside the sand was a bottle. They felt happy and glad that they had found the bottle and the bottle was different. And then a genie went out of the bottle. He looked mean, he looked like he wanted to be a mean, nasty monster.
After that, he wanted to destroy everything!

## Antonina Kutkiewicz (6)
St Dominic's RC Primary School, London

# Matthew's Heroes' Hideout Story

"To save the day. Now, let's find the evil villain, wherever he's ran away to!"
"Ha, ha, ha! I want to fight the superheroes!"
They were there. The villain got one of them!
"What can I do? I need the superheroes to help me!" He tied her up with a strong rope. She wished they'd gone now.
"Let go!" *Boom! Pow! Bash!*
"You saved me!"
They got him in the bot, the bot and the villain!

## Matthew Salazar (5)
St Dominic's RC Primary School, London

# The Day Tyler Became A Gymnast

It was just a normal day when Taylor heard *crash, bang, pow*. She wondered what that was. It sounded like it was coming from her sister, Casey. She was practising gymnastics. She couldn't believe that her sister liked gymnastics! As quick as a flash, Taylor rushed to her sister's room because she was worried that Casey was hurt, but she wasn't. Casey was just banging the table to get lunch! "I thought you were hurting yourself!" she said.

## Precious Sami (6)
St Dominic's RC Primary School, London

# Kevin's Heroes' Hideout Story

Superheroes are here saving the city and there's a villain destroying the city but they will find him soon. The villain is making a sign that says: *Plan to rule the world.*

As they are fighting, the villain hurts a hero and then he is knocked out. Also, he traps her in a glass box that she can't get out of. The superheroes come and save her, then the villain is trapped. Everyone is cheering at them because they are real heroes!

## Kevin Prince Lopes (7)

St Dominic's RC Primary School, London

# Isaac's Heroes' Hideout Story

One day, a fantastic group of heroes found out that Brain Master was going to rule the world. Next, they saw Brain Master putting up posters about ruling the world. Then, one of the heroes tried to destroy Brain Master but she couldn't. Brain Master tied her up aggressively and locked her up, then the superhero friends helped her break out.

Finally, they trapped Brain Master.

## Isaac Shittu (7)

St Dominic's RC Primary School, London

# Bella And The Lamp

One day, Bella went out to the forest. Next, she saw a lamp that had been hidden. Suddenly, a genie came out of the lamp! "Argh!" the genie screamed. The genie said, "Let me out of my lamp!" The genie fell back into the lamp!

## Kimiah Farrell (6)

St Dominic's RC Primary School, London

# One Story

The story I want to tell you is about a family. This family is just a mum and a child. They aren't ordinary people. They are monsters. I know what you're thinking - what kind of monsters are they? Well, you're going to find out now. Mum has poisonous spots, razor-sharp teeth, nine eyes and her name is Snob. The child has four eyes, fluffy teeth, poisonous spots and his name is Blob. Blob was lonely, even though he was going to school, he didn't have any friends.

One day, he decided that he didn't want to go to school anymore because it was a school for humans. Blob spent a few weeks at home, doing nothing and feeling sad. Snob said one rainy day, "Blob, would you like to go out?" Rainy days were perfect for monsters to go to the playground.

As they entered, they saw another monster with his mum flying in. That was Dazl and his mum Vazl. Not long after meeting up, Blob and Dazl became friends. Those two were inseparable and were meeting up every rainy day. Blob also started going to the same school as Dazl. That school was for monsters, so from that day, Blob became the happiest monster.

## Theo Augustas Compper (7)

Wendell Park Primary School, London

# Gooper-Man And The Alien Invasion

Gooper-Man was on his way to the supermarket, like he always was. Then, Gooper-Man said, "I get bored of doing the same thing."

What, Gooper-Man's sidekick, sighed and said, "So do I." All of a sudden, the sky went dark, there were flashes in the sky. "What's happening?"

"I don't know!" said Gooper-Man. Right then, aliens came out of lots of flying saucers and everyone in the city said, "Ahhhh!" In the distance, Gooper-Man and What saw a little alien wandering towards them. They wanted to run but they couldn't because he was so cute.

"My name is Peter. I won't hurt you," said the small alien. "I thought we were coming to be friends with the Earthlings but the other aliens had other ideas."

"Come and join our gang. Together, we can beat anyone!" Gooper-Man was apprehensive about the aliens so he rushed down to Buckingham Palace to find the Queen but he only found aliens. They had stolen the Queen! Gooper-Man knew he needed a plan. He needed to communicate with the aliens so he asked Peter to tell him how to communicate with the aliens but he was gone.

But where could he have gone? Suddenly, Gooper-Man heard shouting in the distance. "We have not come to hurt you, we come in peace. We want to learn from you." It was Peter so he walked up to Gooper-Man and shook his hand.
Some of the aliens went to Buckingham Palace and everyone said, "Hooray!"

## Jack Charman Hopkins (7)
Wendell Park Primary School, London

# Lost Wolves

In the Himalayas far away, there lived a wolf pack that lived high in the mountains. The leader of the pack was called Fang. Now, Fang was a wise wolf and he had a wife called Undis. They had four pups: Lily, Tilly, Milly and Billy. The rest of their pack was out hunting. Suddenly, they burst in with a massive yak!

Later that night, they had a huge feast. After that, everyone fell asleep, but they didn't know what was coming. A humongous, shiny portal opened up in the cave walls and it sucked all the wolves through it! They all fell out onto the ground of the busy city of Paris.

The wolf pack landed in the house of Mr and Mrs Leaky. When Mrs Leaky came in, she screamed and called the police. Suddenly, Milly, Billy, Lily and Tilly jumped through a hole in the roof. "Come back!" said Undis, but it was too late. The police came in and tried to catch them but Fang had an idea, they could use the furniture to climb up and go through the hole in the roof and find the pups. They all jumped out, then cars started beeping and big bike bells started to ring. Next, they saw that one of the wolves, Ranger, had stolen a baguette. Quickly, they ran to the Eiffel Tower and started to climb it.

Then at the top, they found Lily, Milly, Billy and Tilly howling at the top of their voices. Suddenly the massive portal appeared again and it sucked them through, to another world.

## Lila Cate Price (7)

Wendell Park Primary School, London

# Hosna's Storyland Adventure

Once upon a time, there was a family. They moved to a new house. They cleaned their house. Outside the house, there was a tree. Dad made a swing on the tree.

It was night-time, they were going to sleep. The boy woke up at night, he saw a person swinging on the swing. The children kept seeing it and their parents kept refusing them.

One day, Penny found that her maths homework was missing. Soon, Rick found that his favourite cricket bat was missing. The grown-ups were about to disagree when suddenly, Mrs Warren's stew wok came flying at them! Everybody ducked. Everybody decided to talk to the ghost. They waited in Penny's room at night, hoping that the ghost would come to take more of her books. Right as they were, the ghost came and went to Penny's desk. Everybody was shocked! The ghost was no more than a boy. As Jim and Alice watched Henry's ghost go out the window, they decided to help him out.

The next morning, they enquired about Henry's school and teacher. Once they had found her, they went to her and requested her to please check his paper.

Just as Henry had said, he scored the highest in the class and so the Warren's got Henry's mother's address from the principal. They found her and explained their case to her. Suddenly, Henry appeared in front of his mother. As everyone watched, Henry turned into a bright light and vanished.

## Hosna Moradi (7)

Wendell Park Primary School, London

# Sophia's Magical Flower

Hello, my name is Kelly and I've just found a massive flower! It's so beautiful, it's got a beautiful red and orangey-yellow middle. I'm going to call my friends on my phone. "Hey Hannah, hey Darbie, I just saw the weirdest thing ever, this planet is magic!"

"Of course it is, we can't see you!" said Hannah.

"What do you mean?" Kelly said confused.

"We can't see you," Darby repeated.

"Okay, come here!"

"I can't see you! Just put the flower down," Hannah tried to explain.

"Oh! I get it now! When you put the rose down, you're not invisible! I think that we're in a tricky situation."

"We need to protect the flower. Wait! We know that she doesn't like clowns or dogs."

"I see where you're going now!"

"Yes, we could go back to our normal lives! Let's get ice cream, I am hungry."

"Me too!"

"This will be funnier than I thought."

## Sophia Tuzani (6)

Wendell Park Primary School, London

# The Little Mermaid

Once upon a time, there lived a little mermaid. She was gazing at her own treasure, it was beautiful. Then, she was a bit bored so she started playing in the ocean. She was having so much fun until she noticed that a ship had come along. She was surprised when she saw her first ever ship. She had never seen a ship before in her whole life. Then, an octopus with a hat on came out of the ship and took her and her jewels! She was crying so much that she couldn't stop. The octopus took her inside the ship because he wanted to have supper with her, but then a boy on a surfboard came along with his tortoise and he heard the little mermaid crying. When the octopus got the little mermaid up, the boy said, "What are you going to do with her?"

The octopus said, "We were going to have supper."

The boy said, "I don't think she wants to have supper with you!"

Finally, the octopus gave them the jewels and the little mermaid and the boy lived happily ever after.

## Hana Ikeda-MacDermott (7)

Wendell Park Primary School, London

# The Enchanted Forest And The Blossom Queen

Once upon a time, there lived an Alaskan princess who had a friend that lived in the enchanted forest, which was never entered.

One dark and stormy night, she went to find her friend but on her way, she met some petrifying monsters that she had to defeat.

When she'd finally defeated them, she carried on her journey.

After a while, she found this golden palace. It was so beautiful but she had to cross the enchanted forest to reach the palace. She found a golden key, then a blossom queen came and told her, "The key is to unlock the cage. Your friend is trapped in a cage of darkness!"

Then she found a bunny. She said, "What are you doing here all alone fellow?" said the Alaskan princess. She then found a genie from a lamp and also cheered her up and gave her a very, very special amulet.

She finally arrived at the palace and saved her friend and went back home and told her sister about the journey.

## Ishaaq Lakhdari (7)
Wendell Park Primary School, London

# Under The Ocean

When the mermaid got to the bottom of the ocean, she found treasure in the cave. She was shocked that she'd found treasure! She thought that the treasure was for her until a sinking pirate ship arrived at the bottom of the sea, right where the mermaid was. The mermaid, Sophia, became worried and scared. However, she was saved as she swam as fast as could to a small hill.
She met an octopus. The octopus said to the mermaid, "I'm called Captain Octo, don't be afraid." Then she met a boy who was surprised that he had seen her. The mermaid was terrified because she'd never seen a boy. The boy was surfing by and thought the girl needed help. The boy was scared and couldn't look at her as she was a real mermaid. Captain Octo cast a spell on Sophia and she turned into a beautiful queen. Everyone started to listen to her. Captain Octo, the boy and all the sea creatures did too!

## Yusra Tahir (7)
Wendell Park Primary School, London

# Riley's Screamsville Story

This is Alex, he is going out for Halloween. He is going to the black Screamsville. He is going with his friends, Giberd the alien, Max the monster and Matt the gremlin. He has loads of sweets to give out and get a lot back.

He arrives at Screamsville, where it is dark and smoke flies everywhere and bats are everywhere. There's stuff on the ground, yoghurts and Ribena. He can't wait until he gets inside with his three friends but Max is his best friend. He thinks that his friends are in there but he creeps up on Alex, then they go into Screamsville to trick or treat other scary people. They throw eggs and do funny talents to get sweets.

Now, they are in, they are doing wild talents. They get ninety-nine sweets in one minute, it's incredible! They try to get another ninety-nine sweets, with 198, it would be incredible!

Now, they are having a disco for the best talents!

## Riley Philbert (6)
Wendell Park Primary School, London

# Benjamin's Screamsville Story

Every Halloween in Acton, three old grannies would have eggs thrown at their doors, their gardens would be trashed and full of sweet wrappers. This year, Hairy Mary, Dangerous Doreen and Nasty Nelly planned their revenge. They would use their wigs, false teeth and eyeballs. A boy knocked on Hairy Mary's door. He said, "Trick or treat?"

Mary replied, "Trick," and pulled off her wig!

Another boy tapped on Dangerous Doreen's door and shouted, "Trick or treat?"

Doreen shouted, "Treat," and threw her false teeth at him!

Moments later, Nasty Nelly opened her door to a third boy. Before he could say anything, Nelly popped out her glass eye and gave it to him! Terrified, the boys ran as fast as Usain Bolt to escape the cruel grannies. Happily, the old ladies were never bullied again.

## Benjamin Hook

Wendell Park Primary School, London

# Rose And The Marmottes

Rose lives in the mountains by herself. She is fourteen. Her favourite things are skiing and walking through the forest. She has a marmot pet that she rescued from the mountains. Every day, she goes to school in the nearby village. In winter, she has to ski to school.

One day, while she was at school, a big snowstorm started. The village was snowed in. Rose had to stay with her cousins. The blizzard lasted for days. Rose worried for her marmot, who was left at home on the mountain.

When the snow melted after a couple of weeks, Rose and her cousins made their way up to the house. How surprised they were to discover a big family of marmots living in Rose's home! Rose had an idea. She was going to build a sanctuary for the marmots to live in and play in all year round.

## Charlotte Wolsey (7)
Wendell Park Primary School, London

# Hiyabel's Heroes' Hideout Story

Once upon a time, there lived five superheroes that always saved the day. Everyone thought they were the best superhero team ever.

One day, aliens were taking over the whole city but the five heroes had to save the day because if the city was captured, they'd be in big trouble. The superheroes tried to stop the aliens. They tried to do everything they thought of but they couldn't stop the aliens.

Soon, one of the superheroes got iced because the alien caught her and tied her onto a really super rope.

Soon after, all of her friends untied her and also, they helped her out of the freezing cold ice. They thought she was going to freeze! Then, they captured the aliens.

## Hiyabel Tekle (7)

Wendell Park Primary School, London

# The Genie

Once upon a time in a faraway land called Equestria, there lived an elf named Elfinna. She was very brave and protected the castle from all evil.

One day, Elfinna and her friend Jack, who was a knight, found a magic lamp. They tried to light it but it didn't light up. Instead, a horrible, red, loud genie came out! He was very angry. The genie attacked the castle because he wasn't invited to the royal ball. Everyone thought he was too scary and frightening. Suddenly, Jack and Elfinna appeared out of nowhere and started fighting the genie.

After a long battle, the tired and angry genie disappeared into the magic lamp, never to be seen again. "Yay!"

## Noemie Iva Chamoiseau (7)
Wendell Park Primary School, London

# Albert's Screamsville Story

One evening, a small boy left his house. He was wearing a cape and holding a lantern. The small boy went up a hill towards a house. The house looked haunted because bats flew out of the windows and the roof was crooked. The small boy saw a scary-looking zombie on the way to the pointy, old house.

When he got to the door, he saw a pumpkin lantern and spooky eyes peered out. Inside the room was dark and the small boy closed his eyes. When he opened them, there were three of his friends! There was a Halloween party! The house wasn't haunted after all. They danced all night.

## Albert Clarke (6)

Wendell Park Primary School, London

# The Goo Flood

Once, there was a boy called Tim. He loved playing with goo so he made some clear goo.

When he was done making the goo, he started playing for a while. He waited and waited until the goo was done.

Next, Tim's dad called him to sleep. He left the bowl of goo on the table.

Meanwhile, at night, a dog came and tipped over the bowl of goo! It had lots of goo inside. It flooded everywhere! Tim woke up and looked at the floor. He was so surprised.

Later on, Tim had an idea. He filled buckets with goo. He used things to keep him off the floor...

## Hannah Mondala (6)

Wendell Park Primary School, London

# Phoebe's Screamsville Story

Once upon a time, when it was Halloween, a little monster with his dad didn't listen and went to the human's cottage. He didn't like the human's sweets so he went back to his cottage to get more good ones.

He went up to a really scary house and he knocked on the mesmerising door. *Creak!* The door whooshed right open and the little monster went right in. It was really dark, but then, "Surprise!" It was a dance party and he really liked it, but the fun part was when the candy was falling from the sky and a shiny disco ball!

## Phoebe Faith Morrow-Okitkpi (7)

Wendell Park Primary School, London

# The Golden Knight And The Enchanted Arrow

Once upon a time, there lived a knight and an arrow girl. The knight said, "There seems to be an emergency because a bad guy is attacking our palace." He appeared in the castle and tried to break it down. Then, he shouted so loudly and the king and queen lived there. They came out and the golden knight slashed the bad guy with his sword and the enchanted arrow shooter shot her arrow. They defeated the bad guy and saved the palace and also saved the king and queen.

**Rayan Mohamad (7)**
Wendell Park Primary School, London

# Ben's Screamsville Story

A boy called Laslow dressed in a vampire outfit. He was going trick or treating with his pumpkin. It was dark and windy when Laslow was walking towards the spooky house. He was ready to trick or treat. When he was walking up to the spooky house, behind him was a zombie! When Laslow knocked on the really spooky door, a monster opened it. Laslow was surprised. The bat and the monster and zombie said, "Close your eyes." They had a disco, it was good!

## Ben Wood (6)
Wendell Park Primary School, London

# Kyla's Screamsville Story

My name is Dract. I live in house number twelve. I am going trick or treating.

I am trick or treating. I get scared, I see a ghost in the garden! I feel like something is watching me, like somebody is following me. When I open the door, it won't close! "Roar!" goes the monsters. I am cold, shaking, frozen. We become best friends forever and we have many parties!

## Kyla Davis (7)

Wendell Park Primary School, London

# Jayden's Heroes' Hideout Story

One day, there were some superheroes in their hideout, they were special.
One day, an asteroid fell down, but it was an alien! The alien found their hideout and captured one of them. The alien tied her up and put her in glass but the heroes saved her and put the alien in the glass!

## Jayden-Jacq Garry (6)
Wendell Park Primary School, London

# Geography Witch

A long time ago there was a brown, creepy spider and nice old witch. The witch's hat was as black as a black night, on top of her ginger plait. That day, they went on their broomstick and flew through the wind, but suddenly, the wand fell into the forest. "Down! Down!" cried the witch. They searched for the wand but no wand could be found. Suddenly, out from the tree, an owl had the wand in her beak and she dropped it.

The owl asked the witch, "I am an owl as brown as can be, is there room on the broom for an owl like me?"

"Yes!" cried the witch and the owl flapped on.

They flew over the Amazon. Suddenly, her necklace fell off. "Down! Down!" cried the witch. They flew to the ground of the Amazon and searched for the necklace but no necklace could be found. Suddenly, a cobra appeared and it had the necklace in his mouth and he dropped it on the ground.

"I am a snake as brown as can be, is there room on the broom for a snake like me?"

"Yes!" cried the witch and the snake slithered on the broomstick, but suddenly, it broke in half!

The witch fell to the ground but the spider, owl and the snake fell into a bog. Suddenly, the witch saw a long crocodile.

"I am a crocodile as mean as can be and I am planning to have witch and chips for tea!" He started chasing her, but suddenly, a dirty, huge beast came and scared the crocodile away. Actually, it was a spider, an owl and a snake in the disguise of a beast. The witch said thank you to them and took out her cauldron and asked them to bring something to make the broomstick. The spider brought a leaf; the owl brought a stick and the snake brought a flower. Then she mixed them together and it became the best broom ever! Finally, they all hopped onto the broom and went to the top of Mount Everest and had a party!

## Arham B Nomani (6)

Yeading Infant & Nursery School, Hayes

# The Kind Witch

Long ago, there was a witch who had a little, white, fluffy rabbit.

One day, they sat on their broomstick and flew off into the sky with her ginger, long hair under her hat. She had a cauldron to make spells.

The next day, they sat on the broomstick and flew off into the wind. Suddenly, her necklace fell down. The witch cried, then a green, fluffy bird flew to the witch and dropped politely onto the floor. The bird said, "Is there room on the broom for a bird just like me?"

"Yes!" cried the witch.

"Hooray!" shouted the bird, then the witch's cloak fell down! A dog came out of the bushes and gave it to the witch.

"Is there room on the broom for a dog just like me?"

"Yes," said the witch.

The dog said, "Hooray!"

Then, the broomstick broke into two! The witch, the rabbit, the bird and the dog all fell. A dragon said, "I am a dragon, as mean as can be. I am planning to have chips and witch for my tea!"

"No!" shouted the witch, flying higher and higher. The witch looked around but no help could be found.
The dragon got nearer and nearer. Just as he was going to have his feast, a beast came out from a bog. The dragon said, "Oops, sorry!"
The beast said, "Hey, that's my witch!" The dragon spread out his wings and flew through the sky. "Thank you. Without you, I'd be in the dragon's tummy!"

## Sruthiga Sivakantharuban (6)

Yeading Infant & Nursery School, Hayes

# The Magical Mistake

There was a witch who had a tiny, light brown mouse. The witch's hat was as black as coal and her skin was as soft as a white, fluffy rabbit.

One day, they set off and flew into the forest, but her necklace fell onto the ground. "Down!" cried the witch, so they flew to the ground but out from a bush came a bird.

"I'm a bird as green as can be, is there room on the broom for a bird like me?"

"Yes!" cried the witch, so they flew through the wind again but her cauldron fell and landed in the pond. "Down!" cried the witch, so they flew to the ground but no cauldron could be found. Out from a pond came a sparkly fish.

"I'm a fish as sparkly as can be, is there room on the broom for a fish like me?"

"Yes!" cried the witch with a smile but just as they were going, the broom snapped into two! The mouse, the fish and the bird fell into the bog, then suddenly, the witch heard a roar. It was a T-rex! It was after her.

The T-rex said, "Maybe I should have witch and chips." Out from the bog came a horrible beast, it was soft and sparkly. Then, the dinosaur shook and went away.

"Thank you, oh thank you! Without you, I would be in that T-rex's insides!" Then they went to the castle and had a party and went to sleep.

## Yuvika Thapa (6)
Yeading Infant & Nursery School, Hayes

# Brave Warriors

Once upon a time, there were two warriors called Ella and Prince Charm. They were brave fighters and saved the poor people from the Devil. They always kept swords and arrows for if something went bad. They used their weapons to fight.
One day, they saw a golden, shiny lamp. Ella pointed at the lamp, something was stuck. They could see one foot coming out of the lamp! They also heard loud screams that were coming out of the lamp. Ella and Prince Charm opened the lamp and a genie came out of the lamp! The genie was cruel and he didn't like poor people. The genie was very scary and he had long arms and long legs. One day, he destroyed the houses of the people and had a big hammer to kill innocent people. He was going behind the castle and stomping hard. The king said to Ella and Prince Charm, "Come and help me!" Then, Ella and Prince Charm came to fight with the Devil.
After that, they put the genie in the lamp, then they closed the lamp. Ella and Prince Charm had saved the poor people and they came back to the castle and lived happily ever after.

## Manreet Kaur (7)
Yeading Infant & Nursery School, Hayes

# The Magic Broom

Once upon a time, there was a witch who had a pet dog. She had ginger hair and her bow fell down. A pig got the bow and gave it to the witch. The pig said, "Is there room for a pig like me?"
"Yes," said the witch. The witch then dropped her necklace. A fish got the necklace and gave it to the witch.

The fish said, "Is there room on the broom for a fish like me?"

"Yes," said the witch.

The next day, the witch's hat fell down. A snake got the hat and gave it to the witch, then the snake said to the witch, "Is there room on the broom?"

"Yes," said the witch and *whoosh!* They were gone. But then, the broom broke into pieces and they fell down. A dinosaur got the witch!

The animals said, "That's our witch!"

The dinosaur said, "Sorry! I didn't mean to do that." The dinosaur ran up to the sky.

## Dima Al-Shammari (6)
Yeading Infant & Nursery School, Hayes

# Fabulous 5

Once, there was a group of superheroes. Their names were Electric Man, Radioactive Girl, Motorcycle Boy, Supergirl and Flower Girl. They were all on top of a building when they suddenly stopped and saw a giant robot rampaging so Supergirl went flying and went to hit the mental robot. He went flying into the air so when the robot reached the green, soft grass, that's when Flower Girl came in. She took all of the grass away and ran away. The robot got so angry that with his antenna, he froze Supergirl! "That is it!" Supergirl broke out of the ropes that were tied to her very, very tightly and Motorcycle Boy and Radioactive Girl broke the ice wide open.

"No!" shouted the robot. Electric Man and Flower Girl trapped the robot into strong, hard ice. Finally, everyone came together and fixed the robot, then they all shouted, "Yes! We did it, we defeated the robot!"

## Girish Ganger (6)

Yeading Infant & Nursery School, Hayes

# The Kind Witch

A long time ago, there lived a witch and a rabbit. One bright, windy day, the witch flew through the wind but the witch's cape fell down. "No!" cried the witch. They flew down and they searched and searched for the cape but no cape could be found. Then suddenly, the mouse gave the cape to the witch.

The mouse said, "Is there room on the broom for a mouse like me?"

The witch said, "Yes." So they flew off on their broom. Suddenly, her necklace fell down! Quickly, they flew down and searched for the necklace.

Then, the cat jumped and the broom broke in two! A loud voice was heard, "I am having chips and witch for my tea!" She was worried, then a long beast was seen.

"That's my witch!"

"I have to go now," said the dinosaur. They made a new broom, then they lived happily ever after.

## Gurnoor Kaur (6)
Yeading Infant & Nursery School, Hayes

# Magic Broom

Long ago, there was a witch who had a mouse. One day, the wind blew off her shoes. Down they went but no shoes were found. Then, a rabbit found the shoe. The three of them sat on the broomstick and flew away. When they were flying, her hat blew off. It landed on a big, green tree. The witch landed but no hat was found, then a cat found the hat. The cat said, "Is there room on the broom for a cat like me?"

The witch said, "Yes." But as they were flying, the broom snapped into two and the witch, the mouse, the rabbit and the cat fell into the mud. The witch was flying on half a broom!

A lion said, "I will eat you!" A mud beast came and scared the lion.

The beast said, "It is my witch!"

The lion said, "Sorry! I have to go." Then, they all had a great party and the witch made a magical broom.

## Fateh Singh Hansra (6)

Yeading Infant & Nursery School, Hayes

# Room On The Broom

Once upon a time, there was a kind witch who lived in the dark, scary night. She flew with her broom with her friends Bunny, Kangaroo, Butterfly and Fox. The witch let go of her hat. Kangaroo got the hat and gave it to the witch. The witch said, "Thank you."

"That's fine," said the bunny. Then, the witch lost her bow! The butterfly got the bow and gave it back. Afterwards, she lost her wand.

"Oh dear," said the witch.

"I got it back," said Fox. The broom was almost broken, then it smashed into pieces. All the animals fell into the mud. The witch saw a beast. She didn't know who it was. It was the polar bear! "I want chips and witch for lunch!" The animals came out of the mud and they were like beasts. The animals said, "Buzz off, that's our witch!"

## Asmitha Vasavan (6)
Yeading Infant & Nursery School, Hayes

# Room On The Magical Broom

Long ago, there lived a witch and a butterfly. Over the cold mountains they went, but then her cauldron fell down. "Down!" cried the witch. They flew down. From a tree, a cat dropped the cauldron politely.

The cat said, "Is there space on the broom for a cat like me?"

"Yes," said the witch, then off they went. Suddenly, the wand fell down and flew into the pond. The fish dropped it politely but a pterodactyl came. "Argh!" said the witch.

"I think I am going to eat chips and witch for my tea." Then a beast came out and scared the pterodactyl.

"Phew!" cried the witch, then the animals brought things and put them in the pot. The witch stirred it properly and then a magic broom turned up! They flew to the beach and had a party, they danced and had a lovely time.

## Armaan Singh Bagri (6)
Yeading Infant & Nursery School, Hayes

# The Little Mermaid

Once upon a time, there lived a mermaid called Izzy. But she was not an ordinary mermaid, she was the princess of the sea. Also, Izzy loved to swim.

One day, she was going for a swim and she didn't know that Ozzy the octopus pirate was following her with his enormous ship. Then, Ozzy came out of his ship hammock and onto the deck. He grabbed her and said, "You're all mine!" Izzy started to cry. Out of nowhere came a boy on a surfing board called David. He was very happy to be surfing with his brand new surfing board. David saw Izzy crying so he decided to help her.

He grabbed her hand and cried, "Jump out, I can help you!"

Izzy listened and said joyfully, "I am saved!" She swam to the other side and got her crown. They lived happily ever after, apart from one person - the octopus.

## Aaliyah N Balogun (7)
Yeading Infant & Nursery School, Hayes

# Ayshnavi's Blue Lagoon Story

A long time ago, there lived a mermaid who was very bright and had lots of gold. She shared it with everybody and of course, with her family too.
One day, a pirate ship floated by looking for some gold. The mermaid wouldn't give any of her precious gold to the ugliest pirates. They stole her beautiful crown and even took her! They were very cruel, and the captain was an octopus. She was sobbing with tears when a boy was floating by and saw the poor mermaid stuck in the pirate ship. So the boy went a little closer and calmly got onto the pirate ship. The boy grabbed the mermaid's hand nicely and the mermaid stopped crying. She was very happy to get her crown and dived with the boy. She was rescued, and the boy was very proud of himself because he'd rescued someone. They lived happily ever after.

## Ayshnavi Vinojan (6)
Yeading Infant & Nursery School, Hayes

# Tale Of The Beautiful Mermaid

Once upon a time, there was a beautiful mermaid called Wonderful Wendy. She was a kind girl. Her mum and dad loved her because she was kind. One sunny day, a ship of pirates was in the river. She said to herself, "Are they bad people?" She hid inside the castle because she was frightened. Octopus pushed her into the ship. She was crying a lot. The octopus was happy because he got her into the ship.

A young boy was following a turtle. He looked at the ship. "Why is that girl there?" He could see that she was crying. He held Wonderful Wendy's hand and said, "I will take you back to your mum and dad." Then, he met Wonderful Wendy. "That's a lovely name that you have."

She said, "I am a princess because I have a crown on my head."

## Hibaq Ali (7)
Yeading Infant & Nursery School, Hayes

# Piranuyan's Storyland Adventure

Once upon a time, there lived a witch. The witch had a long nose that looked like a sausage.

One day, while she flying on her broomstick high in the sky, her hat flew away. A tiger caught it and gave it to the witch. The tiger said, "Is there any space for a tiger?"

"Yes," said the witch.

Next, her wand flew away and a snake caught it and gave it to the witch. The snake said, "Is there any space for a snake?"

"Yes," said the witch.

When she was flying, her broom broke! She was still on the broomstick. Suddenly, a dragon was chasing her so the animals pretended to be a monster and scared the dragon. The witch made a shiny, bright broomstick with seats and they drove it and flew through the clouds. They lived happily ever after.

## Piranuyan Ketheeswaran (6)

Yeading Infant & Nursery School, Hayes

# Superheroes' Super Rescue

Once upon a time, there were five superheroes named Flash Boy, Specker, Emma, Vision Boy and Supergirl. Flash Boy was the leader and the rest were his crew. There was a bad person. The bad person was called Badbot.

One day, he planned to rule the world by getting a superhero, Emma. He went to find Emma. Emma was with Flash Boy and it was tricky to get her. Flash Boy saw and grabbed her but Badboy got her!

When Badbot came with Emma, he put Emma in a tube with his power and closed it very tightly and tied her up.

A few minutes later, Specker and Vision Boy came to help Emma. Vision Boy helped by taking the tube and Specker untied her.

When they went, Flash Boy and Supergirl appeared out of nowhere. Supergirl put Badbot inside the tube and Flash Boy closed it.

## Naveen Sasikaran (7)

Yeading Infant & Nursery School, Hayes

# Room On The Broom

Once upon a time, there lived a kind witch. It was a creepy night. The witch had a brown broomstick. She had friends - Rabbit, Tiger, Chick and Octopus. The witch let go of her hat in the water. Tiger raced for the hat.

Next, the witch let go of her bow. It was a frightening, horrible night. Chick ran as fast as he could and managed to get the bow. The witch was so happy.

Afterwards, the witch tied her ginger plait but let go of her wand and fell into the river! Octopus slowly made a splash into the river. Octopus found the wand but a huge bear passed through and all of the others fell into the mud. Bear said, "I will have chips with the witch!"

"No!" said the witch.

Then a huge monster said, "Buzz off, that's my witch!"

## Maheen Saeed (5)
Yeading Infant & Nursery School, Hayes

# Gunwant's Storyland Adventure

Long ago, there was an old witch with a yellow mouse. She wore a black, pointy hat. In the night's sky, she put her ginger plait under her black hat. She dropped a necklace and there was a frog. "I am green, is there room for a frog like me?" "Yes," said the witch. He got on and *whoosh!* They were off. They were going after the mountains but her cape fell down! The witch slid and they went down. They searched for the cape but no cape could be found. There was a dog and the dog grabbed the cape and *whoosh!* They were gone. Then, the broomstick broke! Everyone fell onto the ground. Suddenly, there was a dragon and the witch said, "No!" Suddenly, there was a monster. They put everything in and there was a new broomstick!

## Gunwant Kaur Sandhu (6)
Yeading Infant & Nursery School, Hayes

# The Evil Goblin

One day, a princess and a knight were walking in the woods. They were going to their enormous palace. On the way, they looked at the trees, birds and flowers, They saw a sparkly, shiny, golden lamp on the ground. The lamp looked precious and beautiful. Then they looked away and went on. After a while, glittery powder came out of the lamp and an evil goblin appeared! He came out and went to the left side. He saw a palace and saw the princess and the knight. He ran to them and the princess and the knight were ready to fight. There were horrible noises. *Bang! Pow! Stomp! Crash!* The goblin said, "Argh! Roar!" The princess and the knight killed the evil goblin and he transformed into powder. The evil goblin went back to his bottle.

**Eshanya Kaur Khaneja (7)**
Yeading Infant & Nursery School, Hayes

# Tahmeed's Heroes' Hideout Story

Once, there were some heroes who always went to the city when there was trouble. They always worked very hard but they were tired. Nearly every time, the heroes had to stop this villain called Brainy. He had lots of buddies. He planned to rule the world. Suddenly, Brainy came and snatched a superhero's cape. Everyone was very, very worried. The hero was tied up in this rope. He put her in a glass cage. He said, "I need all of your powers so I can take over the world."

Finally, two heroes came to rescue her. They smashed the glass and untied the rope until Brainy noticed. Two more heroes came and put Brainy in a glass cage. They took away the powers. Brainy's buddies were too scared to help. The heroes cheered and cheered.

## Tahmeed Ahmed (7)

Yeading Infant & Nursery School, Hayes

# Little Mermaid And The Smart Boy

Once upon a time, there lived a beautiful mermaid. She lived in a coral. In the coral, there was a beautiful crown.

One day, the mermaid saw a pirate ship. The mermaid was frightened. The pirates were cruel. The cruel, foolish pirates took the mermaid and the crown. The mermaid was worried. The pirates were happy because they'd got the crown and the mermaid.

A little boy came that way. He saw a mermaid. The mermaid shouted, "Help! Help!" The boy decided to help the mermaid. The boy saved the mermaid and the crown brilliantly. The mermaid was happy because the boy saved her. She thanked the boy. The beautiful mermaid and the handsome boy became very good friends, then they played together every day. They had a happy life.

## Akash Suresh (7)
Yeading Infant & Nursery School, Hayes

# The Hunter's And The Knight's Walk

Once, there was a hunter and a knight that were best friends.

One day, they decided to go for a long walk. The knight wanted to take his horse. While they were walking, they found a dusty, old genie lamp and decided to pick up the genie lamp. They were both very, very happy. The genie came out but came out really, really bad and things started going very wrong! He started to do wrong things, like getting a hammer and he nearly broke the castle! It was the most beautiful castle in the whole land. The knight and the hunter were ready to fight and got their swords, but the bad genie had a hammer. It was good that it didn't hit him.

They finally got the bad, mean genie into the dusty, old lamp, back where he belonged.

## Roopkamal Kaur (7)
Yeading Infant & Nursery School, Hayes

# The Princess Who Loves Fighting

One bright morning, a beautiful princess called Katie went into the forest and found a very brave knight called Max. They walked into the forest together. While they were walking in the forest, they saw a gold and shiny magic lamp. Then they walked back to the splendid, enormous palace. After that, a giant genie came out of the magic lamp! The genie stomped to the enormous palace. When the genie reached the palace, it started to hit the palace with an axe and the palace began to shake.

When the princess and the knight arrived, they saw the genie so they tried to put the genie in the lamp.

Finally, they got the genie in! Then they were very happy so they began to dance and sing.

**Simrat Sandhar (7)**
Yeading Infant & Nursery School, Hayes

# The Knight And The Princess

Once upon a time, there lived a young princess and a knight. They lived in a beautiful castle and they mostly lived on an island with sand and some water and trees.

One day, there was a magic lamp on the floor. The princess went closer and the knight went closer to the lamp. They picked up the lamp together. Suddenly, a giant came out of the lamp. He was a scary giant and he was on clouds! The giant was going outside with an axe and was going to chop down the beautiful castle! The giant chased the knight and the princess. The lamp was behind them, they picked it up and put it down. Suddenly, the giant went into the lamp again and they lived happily ever after.

## Rosan Sureshkumar (7)

Yeading Infant & Nursery School, Hayes

# The Kind Witch

Long ago, there was a witch who had a little yellow mouse. She had a hat as black as the night's sky. They set off along the windy woods and the witch's hat flew with the wind. "No!" said the witch. The hat landed on the floor. Out from the bush came a green, slimy frog.

"Is there room for a frog like me?"

"Yes," said the witch, and away they went.

After a while, the witch's necklace fell onto the floor and a snake caught the necklace. "Thank you," said the witch. The witch went with her friends.

"Thank you, I would be in the dragon's insides without you!"

## Khalid Yusuf Mursal (6)
Yeading Infant & Nursery School, Hayes

# Captain Underpants And The Mermaid

One bright, sunny day, a mermaid found a cave and she discovered an orange clam with a sparkly crown inside. As she was relaxing in the sea, she spotted a humongous pirate ship heading towards her. It had a big, black sail. Then she saw an octopus aboard. The octopus was pulling her out of the water, she started to cry. There was a boy called Jake surfing on the waves and he saw the mermaid crying in the ship and surfed closer. Jake decided to rescue the mermaid so the mermaid held Jake's hand, Jake helped her. "Thank you!" said the mermaid kindly. Jake was delighted to meet a mermaid and they all lived happily ever after.

## Varun Sriyen Loganayayam (6)
Yeading Infant & Nursery School, Hayes

# The Five Heroes

Once upon a time, there lived five brave superheroes who saved the day to support people who were in danger. Motorbike Zap wanted to rule the whole world. He was extremely unkind and vicious.

One day, the nasty Zap kidnapped the tiny Owlette. "Please, please, please help!" yelled the poor little Owlette. The very mean Zap trapped poor Owlette in a small, cramped jar. The tiny Owlette felt suffocated in that jar. As soon as the other heroes found out, they quickly rushed and rescued her from the evil Zap.

Finally, Owlette was free. Instead, they put evil Zap in that cramped jar. "Hooray!"

## Parampreet Singh Gill (7)
Yeading Infant & Nursery School, Hayes

# Super Team

One day in the superteam's hideout, Flash asked, "Isn't it a beautiful day?"
So they all said, staring by Batgirl, "Yes, Captain."
Soon, the aliens came and said they planned to rule the world!
Later on, Batgirl was on the street but meanwhile, the aliens arrived and took Batgirl. She couldn't reach Flash's hand. Soon, the alien captured Batgirl and put her in a cage so she couldn't move. Her friends came and broke the cage so Batgirl could be free. She went back to the hideout. Finally, they put the alien back in the cage and lived happily ever after!

## Hafsah Khalid (7)
Yeading Infant & Nursery School, Hayes

# Adam's Heroes' Hideout Story

Once upon a time, there were five superheroes. They fought all the bad guys and girls. "I will plan to rule the world!" said the villain. "I will put someone in my machine to make them evil and stop all of the good. I will put you in my machine and make you evil!"

"No, you won't make me evil!"

"There you are! Now, will you turn evil and make one of the superheroes turn evil to help me?"

"We will stop you and put you in the machine and take her out!"

"No, I am already evil so this machine won't work. I am trapped forever!"

## Adam Di Pietra (6)

Yeading Infant & Nursery School, Hayes

# Kavish's Storyland Adventure

One stormy night, there was a wizard called Jake. The wizard had a sneaky plan to make everyone lazy. He read it out loud, "First, we need some creatures." So he got some from the floor of his dungeon. He put them in his pot. He went outside to get a sunflower but he'd forgotten what a sunflower was like. It was windy, then he saw a ball with lots of hay on it so he took it and kicked and then went back to his dungeon. He put it in his pot and tried it out, then stopped because it was a different potion. He saw a picture of a sunflower, then he went outside and saw a real sunflower!

## Kavish Mohanachselvan (6)
Yeading Infant & Nursery School, Hayes

# Avaneesh's Blue Lagoon Story

Once upon a time, there was a mermaid called Zelda. She had blonde hair and a tail, which was blue, yellow, green and red. While she was sitting, a nasty pirate came and stole her goods! There was a crown, two blue and green diamonds and blocks of gold in a closed chest. He took her! She was crying so loud, everybody could hear her from the North Pole! Then, a boy came with a tortoise. The boy came to the ship and talked to the guards and the leader, then he came and got the mermaid. Zelda and the boy got the diamonds from them and celebrated. They were jumping and playing hide-and-seek.

## Avaneesh Punniyaseelan (6)
Yeading Infant & Nursery School, Hayes

# Secret Lab

One day in the lab, the superheroes were so happy because they had no missions to do. They could lie down on a chair. Suddenly, they saw the bad guy. He was looking for a superhero. He wanted the heroes' powers. He was nearly finished but the heroes came, then he took a hero to the base, where all the bad guys took superheroes. He took nearly all the superhero's powers. Suddenly, the heroes appeared and saved the hero. Then, the bad guy was angry so he tried to capture all of the heroes but he couldn't do it himself. He got locked up by the two superheroes.

## Mubak Omar (6)
Yeading Infant & Nursery School, Hayes

# Talha's Heroes' Hideout Story

Once in a city, there were marvellous superheroes. They were very strong, fast and brave. But once, a scary monster came to the amazing city and wanted to rule the world! He was an evil, genius monster. He also had a few robot parts. Then, *boom!* The superheroes came and were fighting the villain. Suddenly, he grabbed a hero and escaped. The villain trapped her in a metal cage. He also tied her up in rope and zapped her. In a flash of lightning, the heroes appeared and broke the cage. The hero was free! The heroes tricked the villain and trapped him.

## Talha Kashif (7)
Yeading Infant & Nursery School, Hayes

# Room On The Broom

Once upon a time, there lived a princess called Kate. She lived with her bird. She had a pink dress and she had a gold crown with gems on it.

One day, the princess and her bird were flying on her broom and away her crown blew! But, phew! A caterpillar found it, so off they flew into the forest. But next, her mouth fell off her face! A cat found it and gave it back to Kate. Off they flew again. Suddenly, the broom fell to pieces. Kate said a magic spell and waved her magic wand and a brand-new broomstick appeared.

## Mnsy Shafiq (5)

Yeading Infant & Nursery School, Hayes

# Manraj's Heroes' Hideout Story

A long time ago, there were five superheroes and their job was to save the city. They made sure that there were no baddies.

One day, there was a baddy and his name was Blouse. Blouse's plan was to rule the world. Blouse came and Supergirl was there. Blouse grabbed Supergirl with his remote control.

Afterwards, Blouse put Supergirl in jail and she was tied with a rope. Then, the superheroes came and took out Supergirl from the box.

Finally, they put Blouse in the box and was very angry.

## Manraj Singh (7)
Yeading Infant & Nursery School, Hayes

# Take Over The World

One sunny day, Gem and his superhero gang were keeping the world safe from Jen, the evil robot monster. "My plan is very easy, I plan to rule the whole entire world! Easy-peasy lemon squeezy," Jen said.

After a few minutes, Jen appeared and grabbed Chocolate Fudge and flew away to his base.

After a few hours, Jen put Chocolate Fudge in a radioactive freezer, then Robin and Mint jumped and broke the radioactive glass. They jumped, then grabbed Jen and put him in a glass freezer!

## Ayan Ranjit (7)
Yeading Infant & Nursery School, Hayes

# Anastasia's Heroes' Hideout Story

One day, there lived a hero but not one, there were many and they were saving the world every time. One day, there was a robot with a brain and the robot wanted to blow up the world. The heroes came and they said, "You're not doing anything!" But then the robot took one of the heroes and flew away. The robot put the hero in glass and the robot was very, very happy. Then, the heroes came in to save the other hero and the robot wasn't happy. The heroes closed the robot in!

## Anastazja Stanisz (6)
Yeading Infant & Nursery School, Hayes

# Akshera's Storyland Adventure

Once, there lived a girl called Val. Val had blood-red skin. Val had yellow hair and red, sharp, bloody teeth. Val was wearing a blue, pretty dress.
Long ago, Val the vampire went into the castle, then the vampire made her plan. "Fee-fi-fo-fum, make everyone turn to frogs!" But the spell didn't work. She waited and waited. When it didn't work, she added some extra things. She said, "What is extra?" She wandered around, but then when she went, the spell worked!

## Akshera Thurairajah (5)
Yeading Infant & Nursery School, Hayes

# Samuel's Storyland Adventure

One scary night in the middle of the forest, Martin the monster scared the people in front so he could eat them. Martin the monster made the trap hole with leaves so when people walked over it, the monster could eat them. When Martin the monster jumped in, he ate the people. Martin had green, scary eyes and he had sharp, pointy teeth. But Martin the monster was still hungry. He saw a wiggly worm, then he had it for his dinner and he ate it. Martin the monster lived with his family.

## Samuel Adebambo Balogunezzedine (6)
Yeading Infant & Nursery School, Hayes

# Wajih's Heroes' Hideout Story

Once upon a time, there were superheroes called Heroes' Hideout. They were strong and powerful superheroes. The evil sorceress was called Mrs Brain. She wanted to rule the world. Mrs Brain caught Supergirl. Mrs Brain trapped Supergirl and she was stuck! Just then, Superwoman and Superboy came to the rescue! They used their powers to get Supergirl out. She was free! Now, Mrs Brain was trapped. The Heroes' Hideout saved the day!

## Wajih Khan (6)
Yeading Infant & Nursery School, Hayes

# The Marvellous Lamp

One day, there was a knight called Max and the girl's name was Chloe. They went for a walk in the forest and saw a lamp, then they left and went back to their palace. An evil genie called Jay came out of the lamp, then went and attacked Chloe and Max's palace. Max and Chloe went outside and saw Jay so they fought him. Max and Chloe defeated Jay and they jumped because Jay went back into the lamp forever!

## Daniyal Ali Rana (7)
Yeading Infant & Nursery School, Hayes

# Desmond's Heroes' Hideout Story

The superheroes were waiting for a mission to do. An alien monster was thinking of a plan to rule the planet Earth. Then, the alien monster took away a superhero to his lair. The alien monster zapped the superhero into a container. The superhero was surprised because two of her teammates came to rescue her. Then the superheroes locked up the alien monster in the container, where he belonged.

## Desmond Akanmu (7)
Yeading Infant & Nursery School, Hayes

# Moulid's Heroes' Hideout Story

Once upon a time, there were five superheroes who saved the world. The supervillain wanted to rule the world so he could get the superheroes' powers. The villain took one of the superheroes so he got much more powerful! He kept the superhero. But then, her friends came and broke her out and they got the supervillain in the last minute. They saved the world!

## Moulid Abdi Osman (7)
Yeading Infant & Nursery School, Hayes

# Young Writers Information

We hope you have enjoyed reading this book and that you will continue to in the coming years.

If you're a young writer who enjoys reading and creative writing, or the parent of an enthusiastic poet or story writer, do visit our website **www.youngwriters.co.uk**. Here you will find free competitions, workshops and games, as well as recommended reads, a poetry glossary and our blog.

If you would like to order further copies of this book, or any of our other titles give us a call or visit **www.youngwriters.co.uk**.

Young Writers
Remus House
Coltsfoot Drive
Peterborough
PE2 9BF

(01733) 890066
info@youngwriters.co.uk

 @YoungWritersUK  @YoungWritersCW